# 'Twas the Night Before Christmas

Author
## Clement Moore

Cover illustration          Illustrations
## Linda Graves        Susan Spellman

Louis Weber, C.E.O.
Publications International, Ltd.
7373 North Cicero Avenue
Lincolnwood, Illinois 60646

Manufactured in U.S.A.

8 7 6 5 4 3 2 1

ISBN: 0-7853-1364-8

PUBLICATIONS INTERNATIONAL, LTD.
Candy Cane Books is a trademark of Publications International, Ltd.

'Twas the night before Christmas,
   when all through the house
Not a creature was stirring,
   not even a mouse.
The stockings were hung
   by the chimney with care,
In hopes that Saint Nicholas
   soon would be there.
The children were nestled
   all snug in their beds,
While visions of sugarplums
   danced in their heads.

And Mama in her kerchief,
  and I in my cap,
Had just settled down
  for a long winter's nap—
When out on the lawn
  there arose such a clatter,
I sprang from my bed
  to see what was the matter.
Away to the window
  I flew like a flash,
Tore open the shutter,
  and threw open the sash.

The moon on the breast
of the new-fallen snow
Gave a luster of midday
to objects below.
When what to my
wondering eyes should appear,
But a miniature sleigh
and eight tiny reindeer,
With a little old driver,
so lively and quick,
I knew in a moment
it must be Saint Nick!

More rapid than eagles
  his coursers they came,
And he whistled and shouted
  and called them by name.
"Now, Dasher!  Now, Dancer!
  Now, Prancer and Vixen!
On, Comet!  On, Cupid!
  On Donder and Blitzen!
To the top of the porch,
  to the top of the wall,
Now, dash away, dash away,
  dash away all!"

As dry leaves that before
 the wild hurricane fly,
When they meet with an obstacle
 mount to the sky,
So up to the housetop
 the coursers they flew,
With a sleigh full of toys—
 and Saint Nicholas, too.
And then in a twinkling,
 I heard on the roof,
The prancing and pawing
 of each little hoof.

As I drew in my head
  and was turning around,
Down the chimney Saint Nicholas
  came with a bound.
He was dressed all in fur
  from his head to his foot,
And his clothes were all tarnished
  with ashes and soot.
A bundle of toys
  he had flung on his back,
And he looked like a peddler
  just opening his pack.

His eyes, how they twinkled,
  his dimples, how merry!
His cheeks were like roses,
  his nose like a cherry.
His droll little mouth
  was drawn up like a bow,
And the beard on his chin
  was as white as the snow.
The stump of a pipe
  he held tight in his teeth,
And the smoke, it encircled
  his head like a wreath.

He had a broad face
  and a little round belly
That shook, when he laughed,
  like a bowl full of jelly.
He was chubby and plump,
  a right jolly old elf,
And I laughed when I saw him,
  in spite of myself.
A wink of his eye
  and a twist of his head
Soon gave me to know
  I had nothing to dread.

He spoke not a word,
   but went straight to his work,
And filled all the stockings,
   then turned with a jerk,
And laying a finger
   aside of his nose,
And giving a nod,
   up the chimney he rose.
He sprang to his sleigh,
   to his team gave a whistle,
And away they all flew
   like the down of a thistle.

But I heard him exclaim,
   as they drove out of sight,
"Happy Christmas to all,
   and to all a good night!"